KT-579-226

Invasion of the Killer Robots

David Orme

Text illustrations by Ron Tiner
Cover illustration by Mark Duffin

First published in 1998 by
Stanley Thornes Publishers Ltd

Reprinted in 2001 by:
Nelson Thornes Ltd
Delta Place
27 Bath Road
CHELTENHAM
GL53 7TH
United Kingdom

03 \ 10 9 8 7 6 5

A catalogue record for this book is available from the British Library

ISBN 0-7487-3612-3

Typeset by Tech-Set Ltd.

Printed and bound in Great Britain by T.J. International Ltd.

CONTENTS

THE ROBOTS

ARRIVE

In a swamp three hundred million years ago, a green creature lay very still next to a fallen log. The creature was about a metre long. Huge ferns grew out of the log. They sheltered the creature from the sun.

There was a splash. The creature had gone! A minute later, it crawled back out of the water. In its mouth was a small fish. The green creature swallowed, and the fish was gone.

The sun was bright. Usually the swamp was covered in mist. The creature lay half in and half out of the water. The water cooled its body.

Suddenly, the sky became even brighter. Something hot and glowing shot across the sky. There was a huge explosion as it hit the swamp. The water started to boil. In an instant, the green creature lay dead, floating on the water.

Deep in the swamp, a strange metal object from space slowly cooled down. At last, it was cool enough. Inside, a switch clicked over.

Nothing happened! The small spaceship was damaged. The motor that opened the door was stuck.

Hundreds of years went by. The plants in the swamp grew back. The spaceship sank deeper into the dead plant remains at the bottom of the swamp.

Three hundred million years passed. The
plant remains had turned into black coal.

The spaceship was still there, buried under the earth.

THE

MINE

Jack Stone worked in the big coal mine at Western Hill. It was an open cast coal mine. The miners didn't dig tunnels under the ground. The coal was near the surface. Big machines cut it straight out of the ground. The coal was put into big lorries. The lorries took it to a power station ten miles away.

Jack was in charge of one of the giant digging machines. It scooped out the coal in a

huge bucket. It could handle five tons at a time.

Jack swung the bucket towards the coal. The bucket had metal teeth to dig into the coal. He pulled a lever and the bucket dug deep.

Suddenly, there was a crash. Jack stopped digging at once. The bucket had hit something. Perhaps it was a hard rock.

Jack pulled the bucket back. Coal fell away. He stared. There was something shiny there – something made of metal!

Jack switched on his radio. He would contact the mine boss at the site office.

"Mr Wells? Jack Stone here. I've hit something strange. Can you come and take a look?"

"I'll be with you in five minutes," said Mr Wells.

Jack jumped down from his digger. He walked over to the shiny metal object.

He couldn't work out how big it was. Most

of it was still buried in the coal. He looked closely at it. There was a ring marked on the metal. It was about thirty centimetres across. It was like a door into a submarine – or even a spaceship!

Inside the spaceship three hundred million year old machinery started working.

Jack's bucket had unstuck the door motor.

The door started to open.

THE DOOR

OPENS

The metal circle was moving! It slid slowly to one side.

"Get back!" yelled Mr Wells. "It might be a bomb from the war!"

Mr Wells and Jack ran back and hid behind the digger. Mr Wells called his office on the radio.

"We might have a bomb here. Call the police."

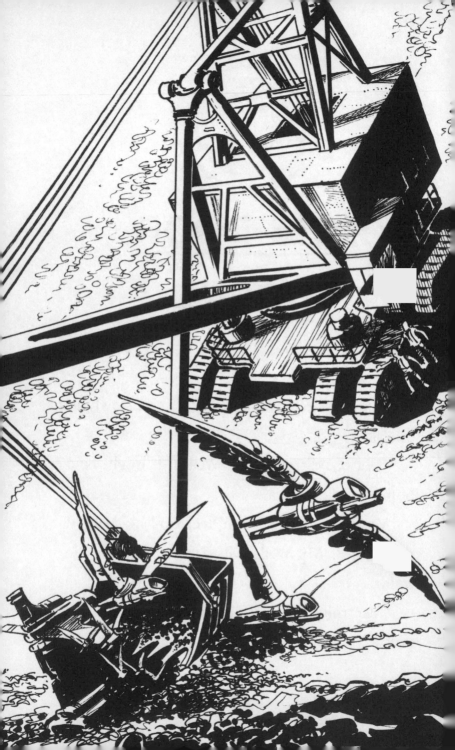

Inside the spaceship, things were happening! Tiny machine creatures woke up from their long sleep. They were the size of birds. They looked like birds, too. They had shining metal wings, and one bright eye.

The first flying robot came out of the spaceship. It flew into the air and started to circle round. Jack and Mr Wells were amazed. They had never seen anything like it.

Another flying machine came out of the ship, then another.

"Let's get out of here!" whispered Mr Wells.

The two men ran towards Mr Wells' car. Jack got there first. He jumped in. He looked back. The flying creatures saw Mr Wells! They buzzed towards him.

"Hurry up! They've seen you!" shouted Jack.

The machines flew at Mr Wells like angry bees. One of them fired a tiny dart. It hit Mr

Wells in the neck. He yelled in pain, then slowly sank to the ground.

Jack started up the car and set off. The machines were following him! He wound up the windows. They buzzed round the car but couldn't get in. They turned and flew back towards the spaceship. Jack rushed into the office. He put out a general alert on the radio to the other workers.

"Stay in your cabs! And keep the windows closed!"

THE

BOMBER

Two days had passed since the spaceship had opened. The mine was sealed off. Soldiers in tanks were all around the spaceship.

The flying robots were seen flying miles from their ship. News of them had been on radio and television. People were terrified. They stayed indoors with their windows closed.

Two more people were killed. One woman had seen a killing right outside her window. A

neighbour was getting in the washing. A flying robot fired a poison dart. The neighbour had fallen. The robot landed on the body. It pushed a needle down into the neck of the dead body. Then it flew back to the spaceship.

A scientist was on television.

"The flying machine must have been taking blood samples," he said. "They are trying to find out about us."

Near the spaceship the soldiers watched and

waited. They watched the spaceship carefully. It had changed since Jack had first found it. The metal was shiny then. Now it was red and rusty.

At last the government decided what to do. They would bomb the minc! The soldiers moved back. A powerful bomber took off.

The pilot looked down. "Soon be there," he said.

There was a buzzing sound behind him. One of the flying machines had got into the plane!

The soldiers on the ground watched in horror as the plane spun out of control. There was a huge explosion as it hit the ground.

"At least I'm safe here in this tank," thought one of the soldiers.

He was wrong. The flying machines were outside, burning their way in with tiny flames.

WILL THEY BE

BACK?

Jack Stone was in his home, three miles away from the mine. His wife had wanted to move away from the danger. Jack was packing up the car, ready to move out. It was raining. He was getting soaked.

Suddenly, he heard a buzzing coming from the sky. He rushed into the house and shut the door. Jack pushed his family into the living room.

"Keep quiet!" he said. "That scientist said that they can hear us."

Mrs Stone gasped. "I've left the kitchen window open!" she said.

"Stay here!" hissed Jack.

Jack opened the door. He went into the kitchen. The window was open. He stopped. Lying on the floor was a flying machine!

It was not like the ones Jack had first seen. It was rusty, like the spaceship. The wings had holes in them. It buzzed, for a minute, then stopped. Its little shining eye went out.

Scientists managed to look at the flying creatures before they rusted away completely.

"Acid rain," said the scientist. "We should have guessed when the spaceship went rusty."

There was one thing the scientist didn't tell anyone. He had managed to look into the spaceship before it rusted away. He had seen a powerful radio. Could the metal creatures have

sent a message back to their home planet? Were the people who built the ship still around after three hundred million years?

Would they be back?